MW00634302

SPOTTING DIFFERENCES

Cricket or Grasshopper?

by Mari Schuh

BELLWETHER MEDIA • MINNEAPOLIS, MN

Blastoff! Readers are carefully developed by literacy experts to build reading stamina and move students toward fluency by combining standards-based content with developmentally appropriate text.

Level 1 provides the most support through repetition of high-frequency words, light text, predictable sentence patterns, and strong visual support.

Level 2 offers early readers a bit more challenge through varied sentences, increased text load, and text-supportive special features.

Level 3 advances early-fluent readers toward fluency through increased text load, less reliance on photos, advancing concepts, longer sentences, and more complex special features.

★ **Blastoff! Universe**

Reading Level

Grade K

Grades 1–3

Grade 4

This edition first published in 2022 by Bellwether Media, Inc.

Library of Congress Cataloging-in-Publication Data

Names: Schuh, Mari C., 1975- author.
Title: Cricket or grasshopper? / by Mari Schuh.
Description: Minneapolis, MN : Bellwether Media, 2022. | Series: Spotting differences | Includes bibliographical references and index. | Audience: Ages 5-8 | Audience: Grades K-1 | Summary: "Developed by literacy experts for students in kindergarten through grade three, this book introduces crickets and grasshoppers to young readers through leveled text and related photos" -- Provided by publisher.
Identifiers: LCCN 2021039714 (print) | LCCN 2021039715 (ebook) | ISBN 9781644875858 (library binding) | ISBN 9781648345968 (ebook)
Subjects: LCSH: Crickets--Juvenile literature. | Grasshoppers--Juvenile literature.
Classification: LCC QL508.G8 S375 2022 (print) | LCC QL508.G8 (ebook) | DDC 595.7/26--dc23
LC record available at https://lccn.loc.gov/2021039714
LC ebook record available at https://lccn.loc.gov/2021039715

Editor: Elizabeth Neuenfeldt   Designer: Laura Sowers

Printed in the United States of America, North Mankato, MN.

Table of Contents

Crickets and Grasshoppers

Crickets and grasshoppers are **insects** that jump. They both have long back legs.

grasshopper

These insects live in many **habitats**. Do you know which is which?

cricket

Different Looks

Both insects have **antennae**. Grasshoppers have short antennae. Cricket antennae are long!

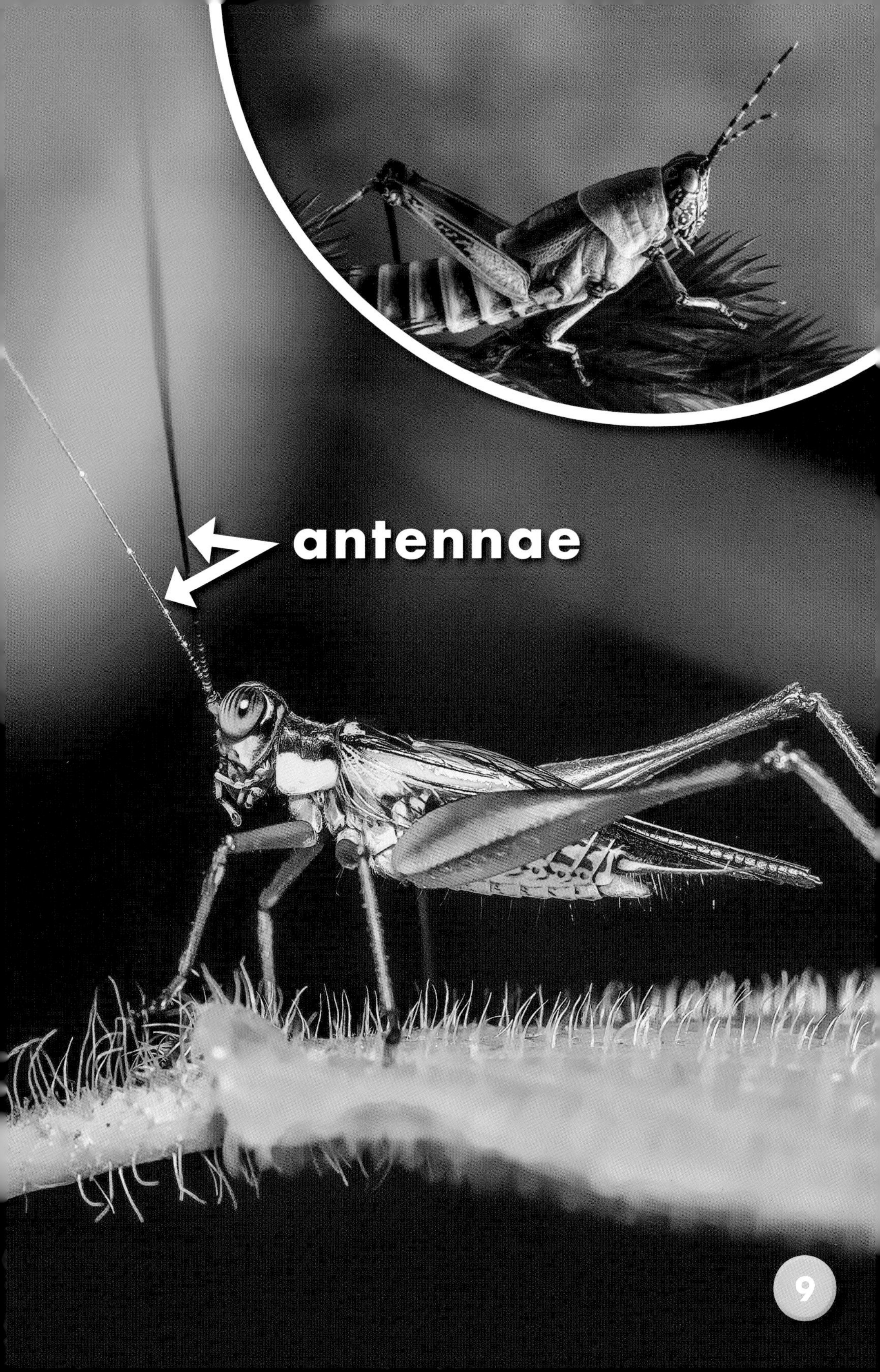

antennae

Both insects are small. But grasshoppers are bigger than crickets.

Crickets have ears on their front legs. Grasshoppers have ears on their bodies.

ear
ear

Different Lives

Crickets eat plants and animals. Most grasshoppers only eat plants.

Both insects **chirp**. Crickets rub their wings together. Grasshoppers rub their legs on their wings.

grasshopper
chirping

Grasshoppers move during the day. Crickets usually move at night. Who is this?

Side by Side

long antennae

smaller size

ears on front legs

Cricket Differences

eat plants and animals

rub wings to chirp

usually move at night

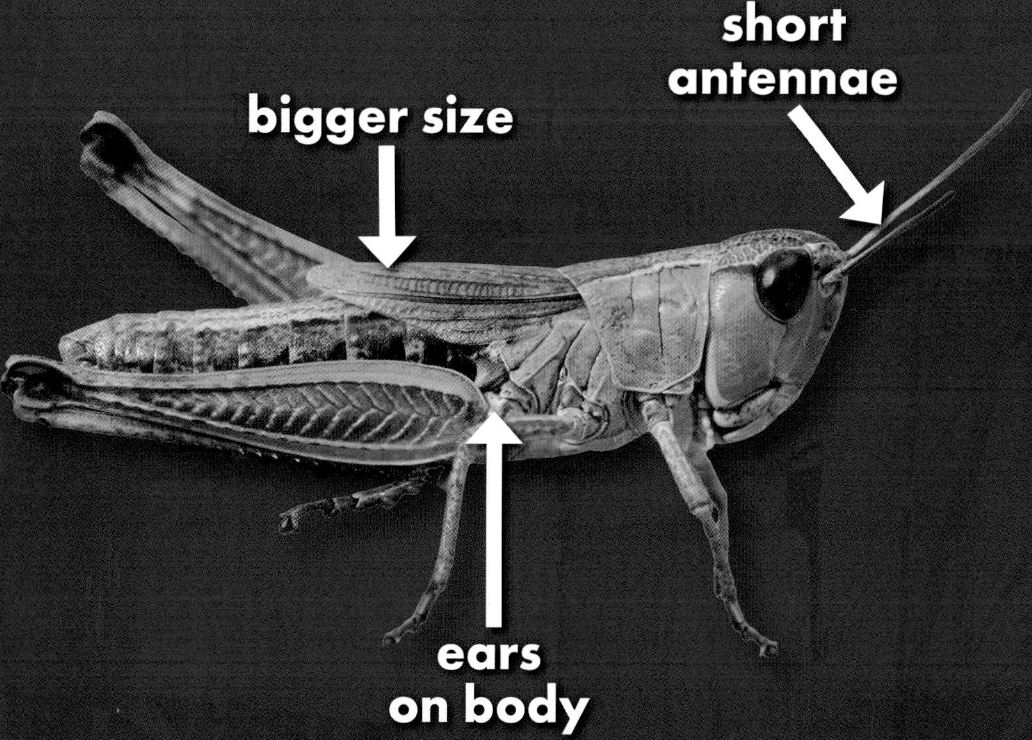

short
antennae

bigger size

ears
on body

Grasshopper Differences

eat plants

rub back legs
on wings
to chirp

move during
the day

Glossary

antennae

feelers connected to the head that sense information around them

habitats

the places where animals live

chirp

to make short, high-pitched sounds

insects

small animals with six legs and hard outer bodies

To Learn More

AT THE LIBRARY

Perish, Patrick. *Crickets.* Minneapolis, Minn.: Bellwether Media, 2019.

Perish, Patrick. *Grasshoppers.* Minneapolis, Minn.: Bellwether Media, 2018.

Statts, Leo. *Grasshoppers.* Minneapolis, Minn.: Abdo Zoom, 2018.

ON THE WEB

FACTSURFER

Factsurfer.com gives you a safe, fun way to find more information.

1. Go to www.factsurfer.com.
2. Enter "cricket or grasshopper" into the search box and click 🔍.
3. Select your book cover to see a list of related content.

Index

The images in this book are reproduced through the courtesy of: forest71, cover (cricket); Ksenia Lada, cover (grasshopper); Nature Picture Library/ Alamy, pp. 4-5; Very R. Wibawa 09, pp. 6-7; Saipudin. Haron, pp. 8-9; Ehrman Photographic, p. 9 (grasshopper); Susan Hodgson, pp. 10-11; Yani Olshop, p. 11 (cricket); kurt_G, pp. 12-13; Russel Marshall, p. 13 (grasshopper); eena Robinson, pp. 14-15; Jimmy R, pp. 16-17; zairiazmal, pp. 18-19; Vitalii Hulai, p. 20 (cricket); www.pqpictures.co.uk/ Alamy, p. 20 (eats); SIMON SHIM, pp. 20 (chirp), 22 (chirp); Vladimir Wrangel, p. 20 (night); fotosutra, p. 21 (grasshopper); Kenz_Hanson, p. 21 (eats); pastorscott, p. 21 (chirp); sunakri, p. 21 (day); HWall, p. 22 (antennae); Nick Starichenko, p. 22 (habitats); encikAn, p. 22 (insects).